Leo's Magic Toybox
The Rescue in the Jungle

Written by Greg Fairbotham

Illustrated by Kelly Malone

FOR THE STORY TELLERS AND THOSE WITH
ADVENTURE IN THEIR HEARTS

Leo loved his toys. Every day he would go on wild and exciting adventures with them.

This particular day was extra special, but Leo did not know it yet.

That morning there came a loud knock at the door.

BANG, BANG, BANG!

Leo rushed to his bedroom window and saw two men
carrying a BIG box.

"Leo come and look at what I have for you" shouted his
Mum.

Leo ran downstairs, into the room and saw this HUGE box.

"It looks much bigger down here" he thought.

"Go ahead open it", said his Mum.

Leo ripped open the cardboard to find…

An old wooden box.

"What is it?" asked Leo, looking at his Mum puzzled.
"It's your new toybox" she said. Leo looked back at the
box, one thing was for sure, it was not new.

"You can start putting your toys in it" said his Mum.

Leo picked up his teddy, Mr. George Snugglesworth, and walked over to his toy box.

He ran his hand across the smooth lid but as his hand got to the corner his hand ran over something.

He looked closely and saw a little girl carved into the wood.

She was wearing explorer boots, shorts, shirt, a hat and had explorer binoculars. Leo traced her outline with his finger.

All of a sudden, the box SHOOK!

Leo gasped and jumped. He looked back at the explorer girl, nothing happened.

He leaned in closer and put his hand on the box. All of a sudden, the little carving of the explorer girl waved! Leo shook his head.

"Did she really just wave at me?" he thought. She waved again! But this time she pointed upwards.

Leo stared at the lid of his toybox. All of a sudden, as if someone was writing, words started to appear.

"Hi Leo, I'm Rei. Do you want to come on an adventure with me?" Leo looked at the writing and then back at the girl.

"Where would we go?" he asked her. More words appeared…

"There are so many adventures to go on but, I need your help with a friend of mine who is afraid of heights. Shall we help her?" asked Rei.

"But how do we get there?" asked Leo. He looked back at the words appearing on the lid.

"This is a magic toybox Leo, open the lid, close your eyes and count to ten" wrote Rei.

Leo thought about it for a second, his mind racing. Then he looked back at Rei and said, "we have to help your friend".

He opened the toybox and climbed in.

He took a deep breath and slowly closed the lid.

He shut his eyes and slowly started counting
"1…2…3…4…5"

He could hear birds singing. "**6...7…**", it was getting warmer "**8**", he could hear wind rustling through trees, "**9**", and water rushing from a river, "**10**".

Leo opened his eyes. Sunlight was bursting through the trees and there was an incredible amount of noise.
He was in the jungle!

Leo stared in wonder at the beautiful sight. He rubbed his eyes to make sure it was not his imagination.

There were so many noises, it sounded like the jungle was alive!

All of a sudden there was rustling in the bushes near to him. Someone was running his way!
"Be Brave" Leo told himself.
Then he heard a voice shout "Leo?".
"How would anyone know my name in the jungle?" he thought.
They shouted again "Leo?".

"Hello?" he called back. There was a pause. Then, crashing out of the bushes in front of him came a young girl wearing explorer clothes.

"Leo, I've found you! It's me Rei" she shouted.

Rei looked exactly like she did on the toybox. She had dark brown hair, green eyes and freckles on her cheeks. She ran towards him, "come on my friend needs us, let's go!"

Rei grabbed Leo's hand and they ran through the jungle. "Who is your friend?" gasped Leo, as they ran across a tree bridge over a gushing river.

"You will see, we are almost there" said Rei. They kept running until they came to the foot of the biggest tree Leo had ever seen. It looked like it touched the sky!

Rei looked upwards and shouted, "there she is!"

Leo looked to where Rei was pointing and saw a little ball of orange fur. "What is that?" Leo asked. That's my friend Peanut, Rei said. "What is Peanut?" he asked.

"She is a baby orangutan and is scared of heights, she is stuck!".

"I'm going to get help", said Rei, "you stay here with her and talk to her so that she won't be frightened".
"Ok" said Leo.

Off Rei went, crashing through the bushes and making loud Orangutan noises as she went.

Leo looked up. Peanut was clinging tightly to the branch and was too scared to move. Her little body was trembling.
"Hi Peanut" he said, "I'm Leo".

Leo saw the little orange ball of fur move slightly, he glimpsed big brown eyes looking at him. They were sparkling with tears.

They were the eyes of a very scared little orangutan. Leo knew that feeling, he'd been stuck before and he wasn't going to leave Peanut up there.

"Hold on Peanut" he said,
"I'm coming".

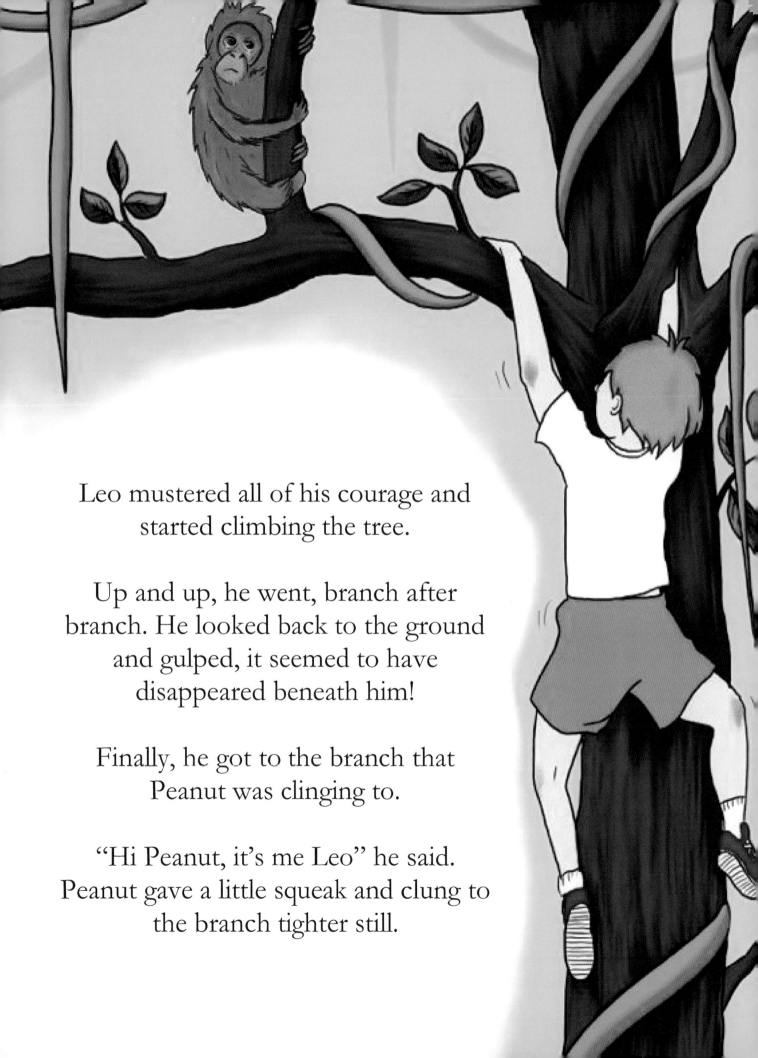

Leo mustered all of his courage and started climbing the tree.

Up and up, he went, branch after branch. He looked back to the ground and gulped, it seemed to have disappeared beneath him!

Finally, he got to the branch that Peanut was clinging to.

"Hi Peanut, it's me Leo" he said. Peanut gave a little squeak and clung to the branch tighter still.

"Don't be afraid" he whispered. He sat there quietly for a
moment catching his breath. He listened to the breeze
rustling gently through the trees.

"It is beautiful up here isn't it Peanut, listening to all of the
sounds of the jungle" he said. Leo gently put his hand on
Peanut's shoulder, he could feel her little body shaking.

He continued to talk about all of the animals in the
jungle and all of a sudden something amazing happened.
Little Peanut started inching closer to him!

Leo kept talking to her about the gushing
river he had crossed and explained about
his magic toybox that had brought him to
the jungle from a land far away.

When he finished, Peanut was sat right
next to him, clinging to his arm and staring
up at him. "Do you feel a little less scared
now Peanut?" Leo asked.

Those big brown eyes gave a little twinkle!

"Let's go down together shall we? Hold on tightly ok?" he said. The little orangutan put her arms around Leo's neck and slowly but surely, they started climbing back down the tree.

Leo smiled to himself, he had never given an orangutan a piggyback before!

As Leo put his foot onto solid earth, a voice shouted, "Peanut! Leo!". Rei came running out of the bushes, but she wasn't alone.

A whole family of BIG orangutans followed her. They made so much noise!

"You saved her!" shouted Rei as she gave Leo a huge hug. "You climbed so high, you're so brave" she said.

"Well, I saw how frightened she was. I couldn't just leave her up there" said Leo, looking down at the little orangutan jumping up and down.

"Well, she is very happy now!" said Rei, as Peanut's family lifted her up into their arms.

"Gosh, what an adventure Leo! We really need to be getting you back home now though" she said.

"How do I get home exactly?" Leo asked.
"Put your hands in mine, close your eyes and count to ten" said Rei.

Leo looked at Rei and put his hands in hers.
"Wait" he said, "just one last look".

Leo turned to look back at the happy family of orangutans.

He looked up at the trees swaying in the wind.

Finally, he looked at his new friend, Rei.

"Will there be more adventures?" he asked.
"Many" replied Rei.

Leo smiled at the thought.

Leo closed his eyes and started counting

"1...2...3...4...5"

The noise of the jungle was growing faint now

"6...7...8..."

"See you soon my friend" Rei whispered.

"9...10..."

It was cool and Leo could sense all around him was dark.

He was sat back in his toybox.

He closed the lid and looked back at the carving of Rei in the wood.

She gave him a big smile and waved at him.

As Leo backed away from his toybox, he noticed that a tree was starting to appear on the side. It looked exactly like the tree he had climbed in the jungle.

He looked closer and saw a ball of fur appear from behind a leaf. It looked at him with big eyes and gave him a HUGE smile. It was Peanut the little Orangutan!

"Wow what an amazing toybox this is" he thought.

He turned and shouted "Mum, you'll never guess where I've just been in my toybox?"

"I've just been to the jungle to help a friend save an orangutan who was afraid of heights!"

"Wow! Really?!" replied his Mum.

"Well, you know what they say Leo, a friend in need, is a friend indeed".

Printed in Great Britain
by Amazon